W9-AAL-413

TEN CLEAN PIGS

An Upside-Down, Turn-Around
Bathtime Counting Book by Carol Roth
Illustrated by Pamela Paparone

North-South Books · New York · London

One clean pig
gets out of the bath.

Two clean pigs drip water in their path.

Three clean pigs take towels off the racks.

Four clean pigs dry fronts and backs.

Five clean pigs powder their noses.

Six clean pigs
smell sweet as roses.

Seven clean pigs
put on their clothes.

Eight clean pigs primp and pose.

Nine clean pigs head out the door.....

Ten clean pigs
aren't clean anymore!

Close this book
and turn it upside down
to see the dirtiest
pigs in town.

Close this book
and turn it upside down
to see the cleanest
pigs in town.

Ten dirty pigs
aren't dirty anymore!

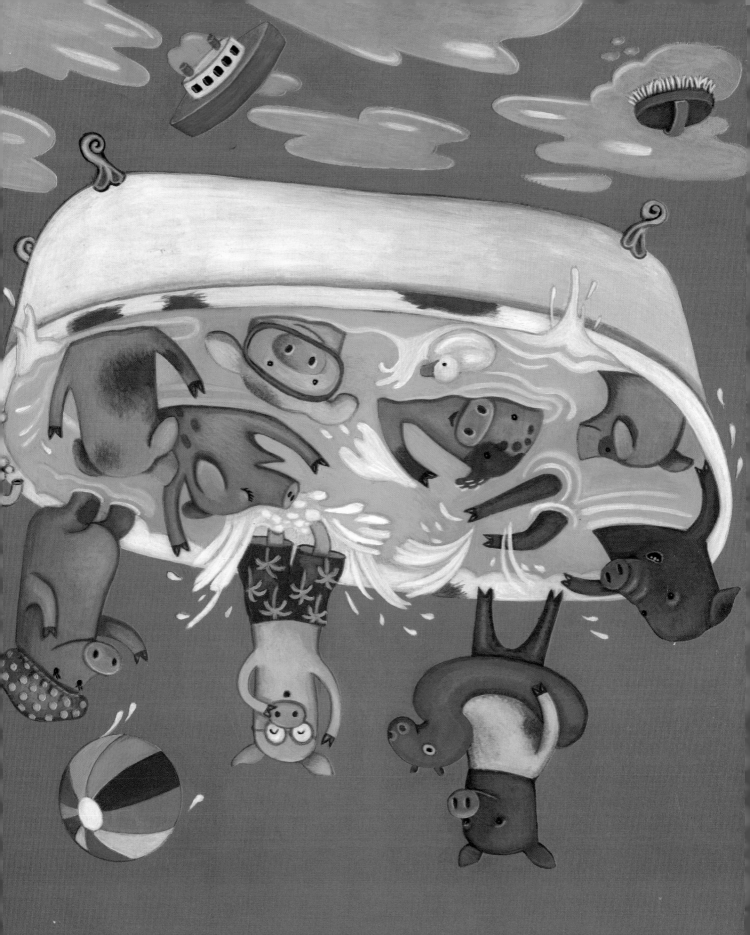

Nine dirty pigs splash water on the floor.

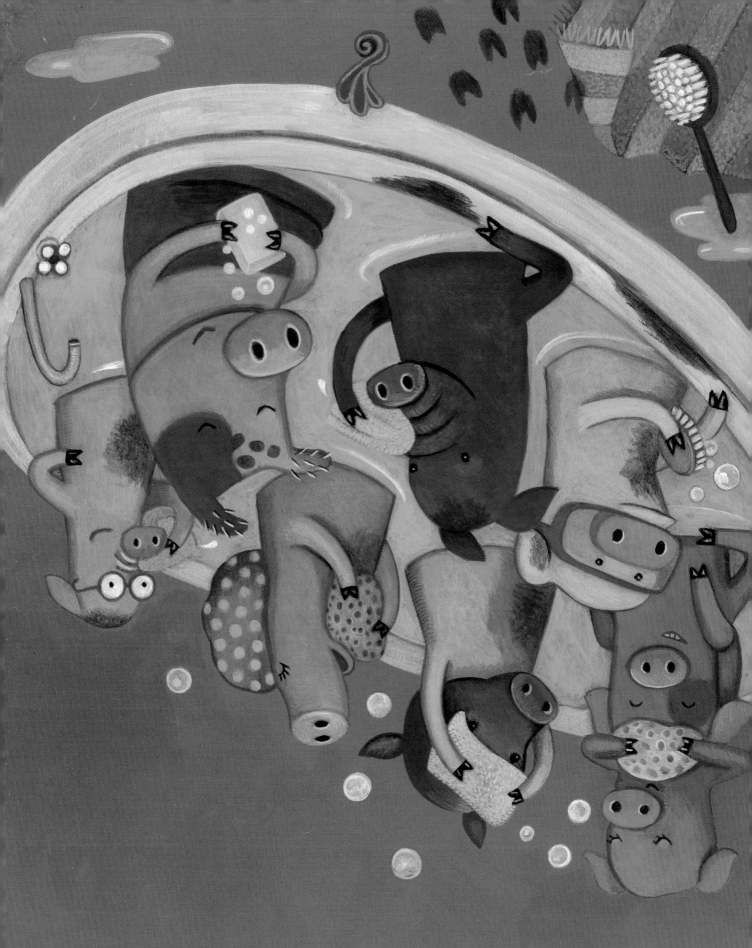

Eight dirty pigs wash creases and cracks.

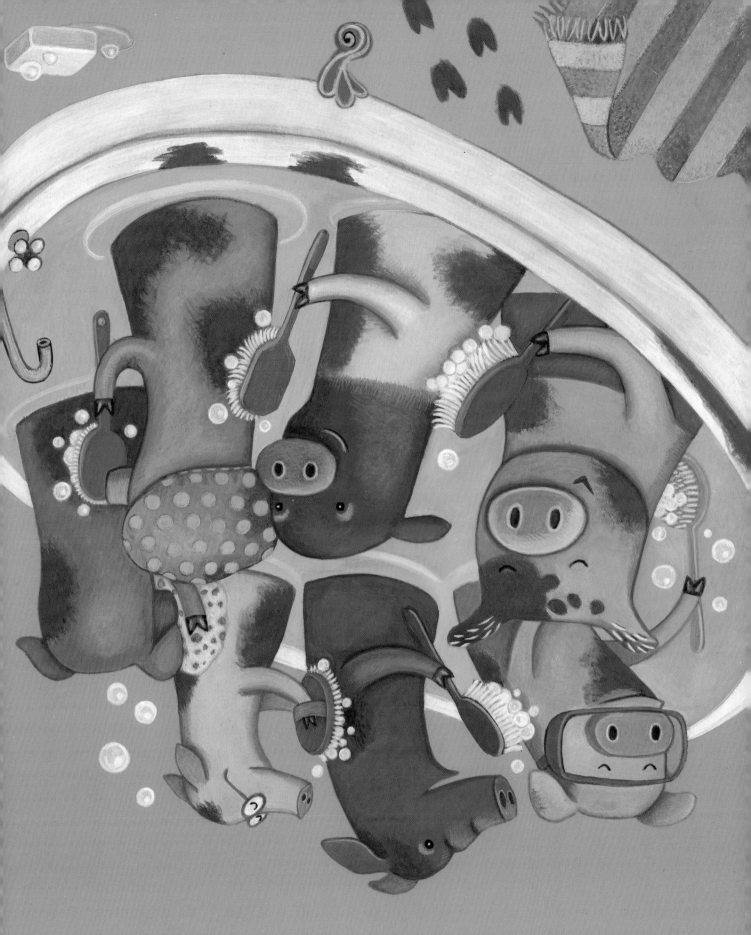

Seven dirty pigs scrub their backs.

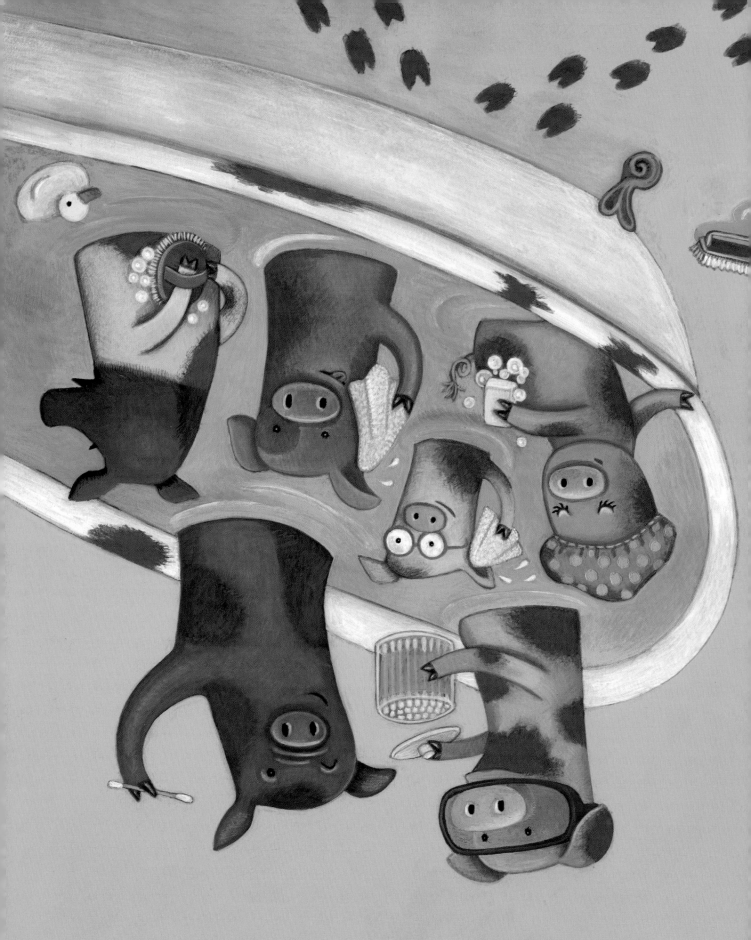

Six dirty pigs clean ears and tails.

Five dirty pigs
brush their nails.

Four dirty pigs
rinse grit and grime.

Three dirty pigs are covered with slime.

Two dirty pigs
go rub-a-dub-dub.

One dirty pig
gets into the tub.

TEN DIRTY PIGS

An Upside-Down, Turn-Around
Bathtime Counting Book by Carol Roth
Illustrated by Pamela Paparone

North-South Books · New York · London

Text © 1999 by Carol Roth

Illustrations © 1999 by Pamela Paparone

All rights reserved. No part of this book may be reproduced or utilized
in any form or by any means, electronic or mechanical, including photocopying, recording,
or any information storage and retrieval system, without permission in writing from the publisher.

Published in the United States by North-South Books Inc., New York.

Published simultaneously in Great Britain, Canada, Australia, and New Zealand in 1999
by North-South Books, an imprint of Nord-Süd Verlag AG, Gossau Zürich, Switzerland.

Library of Congress Cataloging-in-Publication Data

Roth, Carol. Ten dirty pigs; ten clean pigs/by Carol Roth; illustrated by Pamela Paparone.

p.   cm.

"An upside-down, turn-around bathtime counting book."

Summary: In rhyming stories printed back to back, pigs from one to ten take baths to clean up and then get dirty again.

1. Upside-down books—Specimens. [1. Pigs—Fiction. 2. Counting. 3. Stories in rhyme. 4. Upside-down books.]

I. Paparone, Pamela, ill. II. Title.

PZ8.3.R7456Tg 1999   [E]—dc21   99-17367

A CIP catalogue record for this book is available from The British Library.

The artwork was created with acrylic paint

Designed by Marc Cheshire

ISBN 0-7358-1089-3 (trade edition)

1 3 5 7 9 HC 10 8 6 4 2

ISBN 0-7358-1090-7 (library edition)

1 3 5 7 9 LE 10 8 6 4 2

ISBN 0-7358-1569-0 (paperback edition)

1 3 5 7 9 PB 10 8 6 4 2

Printed in Belgium

For more information about our books,
and the authors and artists who create them, visit our web site:
www.northsouth.com

To A Small
World. Thanks,
for everything!

LIESE

June, 2002